Ella E. Warner Stuart

Memorial and Reminiscences of L. F. Warner, M. D.

Ella E. Warner Stuart

Memorial and Reminiscences of L. F. Warner, M. D.

ISBN/EAN: 9783744662734

Printed in Europe, USA, Canada, Australia, Japan

Cover: Foto ©Raphael Reischuk / pixelio.de

More available books at **www.hansebooks.com**

Memorial

and

Reminiscences

of

L. F. Warner, M. D.

Boston, Mass.

MILWAUKEE:
The Corbitt & Skidmore Co.
1890.

To the Memory
of a
Dearly Loved Father
These Pages are Dedicated
By his Daughter.

In Memoriam.

FROM REV. J. W. WELLMAN, D. D., MALDEN, MASS.

The recent and sudden death of Dr. Levi F. Warner surprised and saddened large numbers of people in Boston and vicinity, who not only valued him as an accomplished and skillful physician, but also loved him as a friend. He came to Boston some twenty-five years ago, from St. Louis, where he had had a large and lucrative practice. The main reason of his coming to New England was to improve his impaired health. He soon entered again upon the practice of his profession, making his home in Newton, but having his office in Boston. He easily made acquaintances and friends, and his large success and high reputation as a physician were quickly assured. Yet it never seemed to be his purpose to make his profession a means of amassing wealth. It was his joy to save people from suffering; if he could do that he seemed satisfied. In the last conversation I had with him, not many days before his death, he spoke to me of a difficult surgical operation he had been called to perform, and added the remark that, on account of his poor health he would not have undertaken the work.

but for the fact that the patient was poor and could not pay anything for such a service. That was characteristic of the man.

I knew him well from the time he came from St. Louis until the day of his death, was his pastor so long as he resided in Newton, and was treated by both him and his beloved wife as though I were their pastor, so long as they lived. The longer and the more intimately I knew him, the more I respected and loved him. He was a Christian man, not simply by profession of Christ, but in his beliefs and sympathies, in his spirit and life. He and his wife united by letter with the Eliot Church in Newton, in 1872, and at once threw all their influence, which was great, on the side of earnest evangelical faith and work. He believed in the Holy Scriptures. On one occasion, some years ago, he was introduced by a friend to a distinguished French physician who was making his first visit to this country. The friend who introduced him pleasantly added the remark, " Dr. Warner is one of your religious kind of people, and his religion is of the blue type. He believes in the Bible." As the friend left them, the learned Frenchman said, laughingly, " O, he was joking. Of course you do not believe the Bible. No man of science in our day believes it." Dr. Warner promptly replied:

"I beg your pardon, but I do believe the Bible." The face of the Frenchman instantly took an expression of utter amazement. "What," he said, "you, an educated man, a student of science, believe the Bible? You astonish me. How, for instance, can you believe that story which says that Jonah was swallowed by a whale, when you, as a scientific man, know perfectly well that the throat of a whale is not larger round than your wrist, and the creature lives by suction, and not by mastication of its food?" Dr. Warner replied: "I am aware, sir, that the throat of a whale is very small, but the story, as given in the Old Testament, says nothing about Jonah's being swallowed by a whale." "Why, what does it say, then?" asked the distinguished scientist. "It says," answered the Doctor, "that Jonah was swallowed by a *great fish*; and you doubtless know that there is to-day a species of fish in the Mediterranean Sea, with a throat large enough to swallow not only a man, but a horse." "True," replied the Frenchman, "I know there is such a fish there, but I always thought that, according to the Biblical account, it was a whale that swallowed Jonah." Dr. Warner simply added that many had made the same mistake.

Our friend had an intelligent Christian faith. He studied the Scriptures and tested their practical teachings in his own experience. He was fond of reading the Psalms in German. He thought Luther's translation more expressive and beautiful than the English translation. One day not long after the death of his dear wife, talking with me in his office, he suddenly caught up his German Bible and read in German the opening verses of the Nineteenth Psalm, and his face glowed with delight as he explained the richness of meaning in certain German words, and told of the comfort that came to him from them.

Dr. Warner was a true man. It was his devout purpose, seeking help from on high, to be true to his convictions, to his fellow man, and to God. In his disposition he was genial, cheerful, hopeful and full of kindness. By nature, as well as on Christian principle, he was eminently a social man. His native and ready wit, and his exhaustless fund of anecdote and story, made his company a delight. He was fond of the society of Christian people, and especially of Christian ministers. His pastor and many other ministers were continually indebted to him for gifts and acts of kindness. When called to render medical service to them or their families, he never would accept pay. He understood ministers, and was quick to give them sympathy in both their joys and trials. He was a true friend.

Hardly anything was more abhorrent to him than the character of one who could be false in friendship. He would rather die for a friend than be untrue to him or wrong him. It was because he was such a true man and true friend, that large numbers of people became personally attached to him. He was emphatically "the beloved physician."

The loss of his wife was an almost insupportable grief to him. He could not recover from the shock. They were "lovely and pleasant in their lives, and in their death they were not divided." Not many weeks before he left us, he remarked to a friend that his health was failing, that several times he had suddenly become unconscious. "I know," he said, "what that means. I shall not live long." His whole tone and manner, as he was saying these things, did not betray the least anxiety or depression of spirits; they were rather expressions of joyful anticipations and exultant hopes. He spoke of his speedy departure as if he knew whom he had believed, and that glorious and blessed experiences were just before him. He spoke of his dear wife. Indeed, she, as well as his Lord and Saviour, seemed to be in his thought in all that conversation. He has gone to be with her and with Him. He remarked, "All will be well!"

Yes, good man, true friend, beloved physician, loving husband and father. It is all well.

The following was repeated at the funeral of Dr. Warner, by Rev. D. W. Kilburn, Boston:

"No, no, it is not dying
    To go unto our God;
This gloomy earth forsaking,
Our journey taking,
    Along the starry road.

No, no, it is not dying,
    Heaven's citizen to be,
A crown immortal wearing,
And rest unbroken sharing,
    From care and conflict free.

No, no, it is not dying,
    The Shepherd's voice to know!
His sheep he ever leadeth,
His peaceful flock he feedeth,
    Where living pastures grow.

No, no, it is not dying
    To wear a lordly crown;
Among God's people dwelling,
The glorious triumph swelling,
    Of Him whose sway we own."

"It is not death to die—
    To leave this weary road,
And 'mid the brotherhood on high,
    To be at home with God.

It is not death to close
   The eye long dimmed by tears,
And wake in glorious repose,
   To spend eternal years.

It is not death to bear
   The wrench that sets us free
From dungeon chains—to breath the air
   Of boundless liberty.

It is not death to fling
   Aside this sinful dust,
And rise on strong, exultant wing,
   To live among the just.

Jesus, thou Prince of Life !
   Thy chosen cannot die :
Like Thee they conquer in the strife,
   To reign with Thee on high."

"There is no death : The stars go down,
   To rise upon some fairer shore ;
And bright in Heaven's jewelled crown,
   They shine forevermore.

There is no death : An angel form
   Walks o'er the earth with silent tread ;
He bears our best loved things away,
   And then we call them 'dead.'

Born unto that undying life,
   They leave us but to come again ;
With joy we welcome them—the same,
   Except in sin and pain.

And ever near us, though unseen,
 The dear immortal spirits tread !
For all the boundless universe is life,
 There are no dead."

FROM D. W. KILBURN, BOSTON.

It had been my great pleasure to be intimately acquainted with Dr. L. F. Warner, an acquaintance which ripened into warmest friendship. As a physician well known and eminent in his profession I may not speak, for his associates can speak for him in this department of his work more intelligently than I can. I would say a word regarding those characteristics which were most manifest to those nearest to him in earthly companionship. Dr. Warner was eminently a cheerful man, his greetings always warm-hearted and sincere. He seemed constantly overflowing with good humor, which was contagious. No one could be long with him without being impressed with his warm-hearted, cordial kindness. His action and method were free from everything looking like formality. Beneath that which was buoyant and mirthful there was the individual soul life of a true and earnest Christian. Eternal verities were indeed a reality to him. In the presence of death he had often stood, coming forth to tell with tears of joy of the triumphs of Christian faith. With most touching tenderness and singular devotion he ministered with untiring energy to the growing weakness of his wife, resorting to all methods known to medical skill to hold her back, if possible, that the companionship might not be broken. The painful separation came, but it could not be long, for there came to him a beckoning from the better land which he could not and would not resist, and albeit he moved for a time with a cheerful courage amid earthly surroundings, his tear-dimmed eyes revealed most plainly that his heart was with the redeemed ones and he must hasten to meet them, and the "Good Physician" went home to the "Great Physician" and to the greetings of those awaiting his coming.

"Servant of God, well done !
  Rest from thy loved employ :
The battle fought, the victory won,
  Enter thy Master's joy.

Soldier of Christ, well done !
  Praise be thy new employ:
And while eternal ages run,
  Rest in thy Saviour's joy."

From Rev. S. P. Fay.

1066 Adams St., Dorchester, Mass.,
Oct. 29th, 1889.

Dear Mrs. Stuart:

Pardon me the liberty I take in writing to one who is almost a stranger to me. But I knew your father well. I know therefore how to feel deeply for your loss in his death. Dr. Warner was the most skillful and successful physician in the circle of my acquaintance. He had what seemed an almost intuitive knowledge of the human system and of remedies to be used in sickness. He was also so cheerful and so gentle and tender in the sick room, that one was reminded of " Luke, the beloved Physician." He was kind hearted and generous almost to a fault. I want to give you one illustration. In one instance he was called some fifty miles to perform a very difficult surgical operation upon a school teacher, who was a stranger to him. On learning the trying condition in which she was financially, he not only refused to take any pay, but also gave her $20, for a nurse. The good man was always doing things like this, which greatly endeared him to all who came to him.

I loved Dr. Warner as a true and good friend. He was very positive in his opinions, and abrupt at times, but always kind and full of good humor.

He had all those social qualities that endeared him very strongly to his friends. I am sure it was in his social and domestic life that this kind hearted man, this cordial friend, this generous benefactor, this man of warm heart and kindly feelings, that his moral worth was most clearly seen. Your father was a sincere Christian. It was very beautiful to see the sympathy in all religious matters between him and his beloved wife, the same hope of hereafter, the same faith in Christ, the same love of the word of God, and in all the Evangelical doctrines in that word. No one who saw him in my last interview with him (a day or two before his death), and saw the earnest manner in which he entered into the prayer, can have a doubt of his faith in Christ, and of his present happiness with that beloved wife who so lately went to her reward.

I congratulate you on having had such a father, and I am sure every remembrance of him will be a comfort to you.

Yours, with sincere sympathy,

S. P. FAY.

19 Boylston Place, Boston,
November 14th, 1889.

GYNÆCOLOGICAL SOCIETY OF BOSTON.

206TH REGULAR MEETING.

DEVOTED TO CONTRIBUTIONS IN MEMORIAL OF THE LATE L. F. WARNER, M. D.

The meeting was called to order at 4 P. M.,
President W. Symington Brown, M. D., in the chair.

The President: We will now listen to the reading of a memorial tribute to our deceased corporate fellow, L. F. Warner, M. D., by Dr. Field.

Dr. Henry M. Field then read the following tribute:

VERITAS IN PAUCIS VERBIS.

How few now remain of the group of medical men who, rather more than twenty years ago, met on a certain evening at the office of Dr. H. R. Storer, Hotel Pelham, to consider the feasibility of the formation of the first Gynæcological Society ever instituted in the world. For the most part, these physicians, whether specialists or especialists, thus brought together, and for such purpose, were already in full tide of prosperous professional business, with reputations more or less widely extended, and all of them were enthusiasts, in the best sense of the word, being heartily devoted to whatever might be calculated to advance the true interests of the science and of the art of medicine.

Among the very few founders of our Society, until but now still surviving, "Death struck a shining mark" when it took from us our late friend and brother. Prominent in the small group met upon this memorable occasion, was L. F. Warner: his personality, his influence, his energy, the wisdom of his counsels upon that evening when our Society had its birth, must ever remain indissolubly associated with the history of its foundation: still more such personal relation has stood out, bright and prominent, like the thread of gold in the warp and woof in the fabric of our organized work through all the intervening years.

It had been the privilege of the writer to make his acquaintance only a few months before: it has been his inestimable privilege to maintain relations of unbroken friendliness through all the years since past: to realize, more and more, as the too swift years ran their pace, that here, that in him, had been found a friend indeed! And as respects the physician, it was an early discovery with me, in my intercourse with him—a discovery which I could the more accentuate as I can lay no claim to personal acumen, to astuteness of insight in most matters or in dealings with other men—a discovery (to repeat the word) which a lengthened and more ripened friendship has fully justified, that there was, pertaining to our friend, a kind of genius of definite scope, a natural gift which, with the constant growth it gained, the cultivation it received, had much to do with his success and value as practitioner and consultant, whether in his specialty or in the broader range of medical service.

This gift, which was, as I believe, inherent to the man, presented an aspect—was prominent in two particulars :

First. He had a native faculty in diagnosis, an ability to see as by intuition, often to look beyond the reach of the eye of other men, to arrive at the correct conclusion in conditions of peculiar difficulty ; in a word, to solve diagnostic puzzles and problems. Somehow, he would find his way through the mazes of the labyrinth, although he held not the thread in hand.

Again, Dr. Warner showed a broader range in control of therapeutic measures, an ingenious power in combination, an ability to meet the exceptional wants of a patient, superior to anything I ever remember to have encountered in a medical man who had not made therapeutics a specialty. In repeated experience with him I was reminded, as respects this quality, of the late Professor Edw. H. Clarke. The physician in attendance might feel assured that he had covered the entire ground, in the treatment of his case, that no measure concerned with the relief or comfort, or bearing upon the possible cure of his patient, had been overlooked: but, if Professor Clarke were the consultant, ten or more years ago, or if Dr. Warner were the consultant ten or more years since, pretty surely something else would be suggested: in entire harmony with previous therapeusis, but so apposite, so obvious upon mention, and yet not thought of by the attending physician, however able had been his treatment hitherto.

Finally, of Dr. Warner as a man, I hardly trust myself to speak: I was too much his friend for candid judgment, and we have neither space nor time to give justice to such a theme. Surely we, who have been his fellows in the Society, can never forget his many noble qualities. Was he occasionally brusque, abrupt in speech, aggressive in argument? If so, such method partly pertained to mannerism simply: but chiefly it pertained to a defence of what he conceived to be the truth (this as concerns argument) because of his simple, unmixed, hearty love of the truth. We shall always respect him for his high standard in medical ethics, his pronounced esprit de corps; nay more, his faithful adherence to the claims of the golden rule, which made him, to such as really knew him, not so much a neighboring practitioner as a brother in medicine! And now that he has gone, now that the familiar face and form shall be seen among us no more, that the hearty greeting, the earnest and true grasp of the hand belong to the past and can be cherished only in memory, now that he has passed beyond the inevitable, the unreturnable "bourne," is it not right and appropriate that we should thank God for our Brother's religious faith, for his exemplary Christian life; while we rejoice in the assurance that he was ready for that solemn call which came to him and which yet awaits us all. Thank God that he rests from his labors while still his influence remains and his works shall follow him.

HENRY M. FIELD.

The President: We will now listen to a paper upon the same subject by Dr. Wheeler.

Dr. William G. Wheeler then said:

Mr. President: I wish to mention, first, a matter of business, with reference to this portrait here in the room. I received a note from Mrs. Stuart, the daughter of Dr. Warner, stating that she would like to donate to this Society a crayon of her father, and would send it here to the rooms. She wished me to present it to the Society, and hoped that it would always find a place on our walls. I told her that I would make the presentation. This portrait is one that was made from a photograph taken within, perhaps, two years of the present time. I thought it was proper that this matter should come up at the present time.

The President: I think it would be quite appropriate. If any gentleman has any remarks to make on this valuable gift received from Mrs. Stuart, he is now in order.

Dr. Charles W. Stevens—Mr. President: I move that a vote of thanks of the Society be given to this lady for her excellent and beautiful present.

The motion was seconded by Dr. Wheeler, and unanimously carried.

Dr. William G. Wheeler then read the following paper:

Mr. President: I would add a few words, as my mite, to what has already been said—and so well said here to-day.

The paper that I have to read will be brief and relating more to the early period of the doctor's life than to any other. It was in the early part of Octo-

ber, in the year of 1842, that I had the good fortune
to meet with our late friend and Fellow, Dr. L. F.
Warner. It so chanced that we were members of
the same class that came together that fall and winter in the medical department of "Hobart College,"
located in the village of Geneva, on the borders of
Seneca Lake, in western New York. It so happened that our rooms were under the same roof,
with our friends and fellow-students all striving
and each toiling for a diploma as a passport to the
"golden Temple of Fame." Thus when less than
twenty years of age we came together. As I now
turn back in memory to our student life, I think of
him as an industrious worker, full of fun and activ-
ity, not always in the line of hard or continuous
study : but his mind was so keen and quick that he
would often give the answer, hardly conscious of the
steps by which he arrived at his conclusion. And
when we were in the quiz-room, he would almost
always so manage as to have the last word if not
the last question, and would thus end up the quiz
with some comic story, or perhaps play some practical joke on some sleepy student : oftentimes some
of his best friends were the victims.

But later on comes, as a matter of course, grad-
uation day, the most eventful day in the calendar of
every student's life. This being over, the ceremony

of leave-taking at an end, our late friend and Fellow turned his face toward the West: and I, with fear and trembling, turned my steps toward the East.

The young city of Chicago was then the tempting field for professional ambition. Our friend entered the arena with hope and confidence. But, after some eight or ten years of struggle, with varied success and disaster, he concluded that Chicago was not the Paradise for him. A change of base or location became a necessity. But still the Star of Empire pointed toward the setting sun, and he moved some farther to the west, a little to the south, fixing upon the city of St. Louis as his future home and a more promising field for his work. In this change he was more fortunate; circumstances brought him friends and reputation, so that success rewarded him on every side for a period of about three years.

But then a change came over the spirit of the times, and our friend and Fellow found that public opinion, on every side of him, was widely at variance with his own strong Union sentiments which he had not failed to express on all occasions.

Thus perplexed in mind, with gradual failure of his good health (from malarial causes) he turned his steps towards the East, and selected Boston as his last home. And soon we hear of him as associated in business with Dr. H. R. Storer of this city.

To the members of this society, of which he was one of the original founders, I feel that I need say but little as to his general characteristics as a man or as a physician.

First. As a man, let me say that he inherited a nervo-sanguinous temperament, which gave him a positive nature.

Second. In politics he held to a broad conservatism, and had faith in the Democracy for the ruling spirit of this government.

Third. He held positive religious views, and could defend them, also, giving good reasons for the faith within him.

Fourth. In medicine, he was a specialist,—a good, practical Gynæcologist.

Fifth. He did not believe in self-limitation of disease or expectancy in its plan of treatment. He was opposed to new theories and would often puncture the air bubbles that might float within his reach.

Sixth. He had confidence in a few important drugs, and these he applied with wonderful skill. For instance, small doses of Calomel, large doses of Quinine and Iodide of Potassium, not omitting the "hot water douche" and the internal application of the Tinct. of Iodine to the internal cavity of the uterus.

Many of these personal traits, which were intensified in his later years, we saw in his youth and in his student life; or, in other words, we saw in the boy of twenty the very man of fifty to seventy.

In closing, let me say that he carried the same qualities of heart and mind all through life; and that his many friends and patients all felt the gentleness of his nature, as well as the sunny influence of his genial smiles and kind words of encouragement when he was called to minister at the bedside of suffering and pain.

W. G. WHEELER, M. D.

The President: Dr. Marcy has some remarks to make, gentlemen, and you will now listen to him.

Dr. Henry O. Marcy.—Mr. President and members of the Society: When I was asked if I would say something at this meeting, in remembrance of our mutual old friend, I deemed it wiser that what I should have to say I should offer to you from manuscript.

I esteem it a privilege to bear testimony to the character and worth of our late distinguished member, Dr. Warner, to whose memory this meeting is devoted. The enthusiasm and zeal which was born of the teachings of Dr. H. R. Storer had not alone made of me his devoted pupil for some years, but had sent me abroad during the years of 1869 and 1870 in the special pursuance of gynæcological study. Early upon my return from Europe, I was presented to Dr. Warner, who had recently associated himself with Dr. Storer in Boston, being unable longer to continue the practice of medicine in St. Louis (for physical reasons). Our acquaintance ripened into friendship. Through his personal influence I became early a member of this Society. I shall ever be especially grateful for the services which were rendered me by Dr. Warner at an early date, in introducing me favorably to the members of the American Medical Association. The genial doctor appeared to know every one, was rarely at a loss for a name and something of individual history, assuring each and all alike that he wanted them to become acquainted with his young friend Dr. Marcy, and this at a time when, for special reasons, it seemed a necessity that I should seek a wider association with the profession in America. Such service was invaluable. I have the satisfaction of knowing, also, that one or more of the important offices tendered to me in the Association came through his influence.

Although Dr. Warner is best known as the genial, enthusiastic, fun-loving, story-telling companion, we are all of us none the less aware of his stern and sturdy convictions, which he oftentimes gave expression to in a positive and unique manner. The members of this Society will remember that in this sense Dr. Warner was often in disagreement with my own views and opinions upon medical subjects, to which he never hesitated to give expression. These differences were never, however, personal; and the friendship of the entire period remained unbroken, until about three years ago, when, through the misplaced confidence of a supposed mutual friend, our long friendly relations for a time ceased. Happily this proved only temporary, and I hold in pleasant remembrance many reassuring evidences of his affection and esteem, and treasure in memory a delightful evening spent with him in my own library only a few nights before he was stricken down with his last illness.

Although ever ready to express his positive convictions upon subjects within the scope of his professional domain, and of which he was often an earnest advocate, Dr. Warner had great reticence in committing his views to writing. Most of the members remember, doubtless, a paper which he published some years ago upon the hepatic functions and their relations to pelvic diseases, which paper evoked at the time wide-spread friendly criticisms. It was only at my earnest and repeated solicitation, when President of the Section of Obstetrics and Diseases of Women, of the American Medical Association, that he consented to write it, and I well remember the deprecation with which he viewed the production, as evidence of his innate modesty. Although he was always able to express himself forcibly and with becoming dignity, yet he had a great shrinking from publicity, an interesting illustration of which occurred at the New York meeting of the American Medical Association. The President of the Section on Diseases of Women was unfortunately detained from being present at the meeting, and, upon my nomination of Dr. Warner, he was unanimously elected by the several hundred present to fill the place. Although the compliment was duly appreciated by him, nothing could persuade his acceptance.

In argument he never lacked in apt and abundant illustrations, as we all so well remember. Only the last time I saw him when able to converse, he gave me an example of this. A wealthy friend had become interested in a benevolent scheme for the endowment of a hospital, but which Dr. Warner believed was established for private and personal motives. His reply was, "Let me see your hands." His astonished friend said, "What, are they not clean?" "They are now. Pitch, however, contaminates. Keep them undefiled."

The long illness of Mrs. Warner during the past year made evident serious inroads upon the doctor's constitutional health and vigor. For a considerable period, I saw him almost daily, and never for a moment did it appear that the burden of his sorrow over her suffering was not uppermost in all his thoughts. He rallied for a little under the enforced recreation and absence from professional care for some weeks following her death, but he was never restored to his former vigor, and seemed to be possessed with the presentiment that he was not long to live.

In the sick chamber, he was ever thoughtful, but inspired his patients with assurance and hope. One of his strongest qualities was the dominating personal influence which he exercised in a quiet way over those about him. His religious faith gave no wavering of doubt, and was exhibited in the faithful discharge of his Christian duties, both in and out of church, of the lessons taught by the Great

Master. Such lives cannot be spent in vain, and in that of our late Fellow we find much to admire and to emulate.

HENRY O. MARCY.

The President: I am very sorry to say, gentlemen, that Dr. H. R. Storer has written Dr. Wheeler and myself, saying that he cannot be present with us to-day. There is no man living, probably, who could have given us a better account of our late fellow-laborer than Dr. Storer. In lieu of his presence, he has sent me the following letter, a somewhat long letter, which I will take the liberty of reading to you. It will take the place of a paper from him.

NEWPORT, R. I., Nov. 6th, 1889.

MY DEAR DR. BROWN:

Did I feel physically able I would gladly accept the invitation you have extended to me through our friend Dr. Wheeler, to join with the members of the Gynæcological Society of Boston in mourning, as a body, their late member, Dr. L. F. Warner. Railway traveling is, however, extremely fatiguing to me, and I am almost certain to get ill upon even so slight an exposure as the Boston trip at this time of the year.

To no one in the Society is Dr. Warner's loss greater than to myself. Our association together, long so intimate professionally, had grown into closest friendship, and this was not broken when, through sudden invalidism, I was compelled, sorely against my preference, to retire from active practice. I ever found in Dr. Warner a most interesting companion. While we were together we differed radically in politics, each morning the "Post" being brought to his desk and the "Advertiser" to my own: yet our discussions thereon were always in the kindliest spirit, and we probably mutually modified any intolerance in each other's opinions. During the first of our connection, we were at absolute variance in religion, yet each met the other's views in a brotherly fashion, and it is in part through his influence that my own previous convictions became modified, and, once tending in his direction, reached finally a point beyond that which his more rigid early education in such matters permitted him to attain. His Western ways of thought and expression,—fresh, sparkling, suggestive, generous, persuasive, convincing,—were in such marked contrast to our own comparatively provincial concentration, our Boston introspection and local hero worship, our professional agnosticism, or self-limitation, of interest and sympathy as well as of disease, that, one and all, we could not help being influenced by Dr. Warner, even in spite of ourselves. Among all the founders of the Society, there was not one whose personality was so marked, so strong, so ever felt, and so consciously recognized, as his. Not a man of us but who appreciated, as from none other, his constant influence.

Was it our venerable, and by all beloved, Lewis? In geniality, quickness at repartee, and the wisdom learned by a sometimes bitter professional experience, he was well matched by his brother Mason, Dr. Warner. Was it Martin, aggressive and at times almost cynical, yet interesting from his profound knowledge of medical history, his skill as a surgeon, and his zeal as an active disciple of Jenner? Dr. Warner was his equal with the broadsword of attack or the foil of tingling criticism, and the men who so persistently courted each other's prowess during our discussions remained good friends. Was it Dutton? Equally versed in the mysteries of life insurance, they could discuss averages, premiums, and the expectations of life, not merely in the male sex, but what was then considered unstable ground, the female also. Was it Blake? Dr. Warner was as versed in Irish history as in that of our own country, and was quick to recognize the noble aspirations, repressed at home, which have here found place for full development.   Was it Pinkham, friend by birth, as well as through inherent kindliness.   Between him and our deceased brother there was, I believe, ever the most complete respect and esteem.   Was it Norris?   No one of our number stood higher in Dr. Warner's affection.   He long saw much of his practice, in consultation, and considered our Cambridge associate the type of the high-minded Christian gentleman, modest and unpretentious, devoted to his labors, not making of his sectarian ties either a cloak for hypocrisy or a mere stepping stone to pecuniary advancement.   Was it Bixby, poor fellow, for whom we all had affection?   Dr. Warner was constantly ready to act for him in *loco parentis*, and was never perplexed save there were recollections brought up of Surinam or Prague. Was it our Dartmouth professor, wise in that art wherein it is so much pleasanter to give than to receive?   Dr. Warner's personal experience as a pharmacist before he began the practice of medicine, then always stood him in good stead, and he could discuss Dr. Field's propositions as one who knew whereof he spoke.   Was it Both, whose sparkling light went out in such darkness?   Dr. Warner alone of us all perhaps, could subvert his theories, laugh at his bitterness, and in private apply balm to his wounds, and cheer his gloom with

words of hope. Was it Dr. Wheeler, gentlest of
men, and skillful as unassuming? He and Dr.
Warner were students together, and it was delightful to hear them recall the mutual reminiscences of
their youth. Was it our distinguished colleague
from fair Scotland, who now rules your delibera-
tions so gracefully? To him Dr. Warner was
bound by the strong ties of national kinship, and
though he might not always acknowledge all that
he felt, he had equal pride in the successes of Glas-
gow training as in those of Edinburgh. And so we
might go on, to the end of our long list. In each,
Dr. Warner found some special excellence, and by
each, I have no doubt, despite any seeming chafes
or asperities of the moment, he was in reality both
respected and admired.

Dr. Warner was to me a very dear friend. I
knew of the hard places in his life. He was with
me in many of mine. To think of him as gone is
very difficult. Quick, sensitive, kindly, sympathetic, generous, self-sacrificing; he was all of these.
Having himself lost, he could comfort the bereaved.
Partially deprived of an important physical sense,
he was the more alive to the sufferings of others,
and seemed to have besides a clearer mental vision.
He could rejoice with the happy,—and mourn with

the afflicted, as one who had himself drunk from the bitter chalice.

I was at his death bed, but a short time before the passage of his soul. It was during a brief lucid interval, and, after recognizing me, his mind turned wholly to our past together. He spoke in the most tender and brotherly way of my own illness, my permanently crippled physical condition, and my having had to retire from the professional arena whose friendly rivalries I had formerly so enjoyed. Fearing that he was fatiguing himself, I begged him not to think of what had gone, and to believe that I accepted my disappointment as all for the best. His only answer was, "My dear Dr. Storer, I am speaking from my heart."

And now it is from my own heart I write you that the Gynaecological Society and you and I have lost one of our best and truest friends. We may well,—singly, and together as an Association of earnest inquirers into truth,—remember him with sincere affection.

Faithfully Yours,
HORATIO R. STORER.

Dr. Wm. Symington Brown, Pres't.

3

The President: Now, gentlemen, we would be glad to listen to any of you who would like to say anything on the subject.

Dr. Horace C. White then said: Mr. President. I had not intended to say anything, as there are so many that can speak of long and intimate relations with Dr. Warner. I thought, however, as I was sitting here while his life was being recounted, that I would like to speak of this one circumstance: I consider it the proudest thing I have to think of in connection with this Society, that, as I suppose, I was the means of retaining him in the Society, and of his becoming an honorable member of the Society. His positive nature and his dislike for anything that was wrong, as he saw it, at one time, as you remember, led him to send his resignation to this Society. Knowing even what I did, I believed it would be best to ask him to retract, and I felt that this Society could not afford to have his resignation accepted. Even after the committee of the Society had been to him to ask him to withdraw his resignation, I went personally, as President of the Society, and told him that I was not going to ask him to take back anything he had done, but that I believed I voiced the unanimous sentiment of the Society in asking him to let us make him an honorary member. He consented, and his name and his presence were with us afterward. The conversation that I had with him that afternoon led me to see the heart and inmost thought of the man. I felt as though I received an inspiration for good thoughts. I remember his noble, kindly criticism of those from whom he differed, and his dislike of those things which he considered wrong, even to that positive degree which would lead him to separate even from his best friends when he thought they made mistakes. I shall ever remember how he took my hand and thanked me for coming to see him upon that occasion. And when I said to him, "I hope this will be the beginning of complete harmony among those who should be friends," his assent to that, and the manner of his assent, led me to believe that it would be, as it soon was.

The President: Gentlemen, on this occasion we are honored with the presence of our venerable and worthy friend, Dr. Bowditch, and, if he has anything to say on this subject, we would be very glad to hear him. Dr. Bowditch, will you favor us?

Dr. Henry I. Bowditch:4 Mr. President and members of the Society: It has not been my custom to refuse to speak on such an occasion as that which calls you together to-day. I am not prepared

—I regret that I did not see the proofs of these pages before publication — consequently I feel obliged to mark the pages of this interesting "Memorial"

to make any lengthy remarks upon Dr. Warner. It has been done a great deal better than I could do it, by those who have spoken before me, and especially by the full account given us by our friend, Dr. Storer, who knew him so intimately. But, as I was coming along, I thought, what was it that made me, who was not a specialist in his department, feel always an interest in him, and that made me always ready to greet him and be greeted by him with the greatest kindness for so many years? And I concluded this,—that it was owing to the fact that he was not in any degree a sneak. What he saw and what he thought, he let us know: sometimes very decidedly, but never unpleasantly, as I found it. Sneaks (excuse me if I revert to that word again) are not uncommon in this world. A great many men are afraid to express their opinions until they have heard what other folks say; for example, one man said to me, on one occasion, that he always thought it best to keep in with the majority. Now, Dr. Warner had no such feeling as that. He let out what he had to say, and gave it with full strength to those with whom he spoke. He was thoroughly honest, and I thought, as far as I could judge, his opinions in regard to his specialty were correct. Of course, I thought he was right when he took my side on a certain occasion when I protested, from my previous experience in obstetrics, that, though cleanliness should be practiced to the last degree,—the tendency was to make too many injections into the uterus, as if Nature had so arranged us that every physiological birth was, in reality, pathological ; and therefore we, miserable beings and puny beings as we are, compared with Nature's powers, must inject, every time, into the vagina or, sometimes, into the uterus : and he took my side when I was retorted upon by some persons, who really ought to have known more about it than I, upon the ground that I had had no experience of late years,—that "of late years they had got new ideas." He defended me on another occasion in that point of view. He looked upon it as a thing which ought to be given up, and I believe it is now generally given up. We must practice perfect cleanliness, but the injections employed in former times to destroy the "germs" have been given up, I suppose. I think he was radically conservative, too, in his methods. I do not think he ever gave credit, quite, to the glories of modern abdominal surgery. I recollect, on one occasion, hearing that he did not approve of such things. When I had come to the conclusion—no surgeon as I am—that in certain cases where there was no doubt that death would happen otherwise, it was important to make exploratory

incisions in the abdomen, he, I think, would have
objected to them, I, at that time, felt that eventually—
and I believe it is now getting fast to that state of
feeling—eventually we, ~~at that time many years ago,
would~~ be considered as ~~being~~ in a state of mediaeval
surgery, not to perform operations such as are
now performed *a few only* with perfect safety: when, for
instance, a man can *open the abdomen and* pass his arm, up to his elbow,
into a man's esophagus and pull down ~~half his
teeth~~, *also by laparotomy* or can relieve and cure a patient by taking out
a gall stone, *upset fastened by a quick unealing draft* Well, I think that Warner would
not have followed with me; yet, through the whole
of it, he would have the same face of kindness and
jollity. He was always jolly when I met him. It
was characteristic of him. And I formed the conclusion that he was one who was naturally conservative and was not prepared to accept the views that
I held. In fact, I think we all ought to be modest
in all our views, and not to demand that others
shall believe in them until we have thoroughly
proved them. When I learned that Warner was
dead, I felt that it was a personal loss that I had
suffered. I have rarely been thrown in contact with
a man who has left such an impression upon me of
kindliness and gentle spirit, and, though I knew
nothing of him except in the most general way, I
regret his loss as that of the most personal friend.
I am glad to be here to say these few words.

Dr. George W. Jones then said: It would not be becoming in me to make any eulogy upon our brother, Dr. Warner, who has passed away, in the presence of those who can do it better than I can, and after we have heard the letter that has been received from his old and intimate friend. Yet I cannot let this occasion pass by without contributing my word of praise to the genial, gentle profession-al brother whom I have met here in the Gynæcolo-gical Society. I did not know Dr. Warner profes-sionally until I entered this Society; but, since that time, I have met him frequently, professionally and in the Society meetings, and in our Massachusetts Medical Society meetings, and have always found him the same genial, light-hearted, buoyant-spirited gentleman, the same kind, generous-hearted profes-sional brother that you all knew him to be. In his death, coming as it has so suddenly among us, we have, I feel, lost a kind and honest friend of the Society; and, at the same time, a personal loss is entailed upon each of us. I will not make ex-tended remarks upon my acquaintance with Dr. Warner. He was a gentleman, who, whenever I had occasion to speak with him upon professional subjects, always seemed to grasp the pith of the matter, divesting each fact of every shell, getting at the kernel of the nut, and able to give some wholesome advice in regard to the subject presented. It is with deep sorrow that I come here this afternoon, to contribute my memento. It was with a feeling of the greatest sorrow that I learned of his death.

Dr. Frank L. Burt: I do not feel that I ought to try to say anything at all. As I am the youngest member in the Society, and, perhaps, the last to be admitted, though I cannot say as to that, I have had scarcely any opportunity of meeting Dr. Warner; and so, as regards anything in the way of professional association, I have nothing whatever to say; I know nothing about the man in that respect. Yet I have met him a very few times. The first was only a few months before I came into this Society, something like three years ago; and I remember that occasion very pleasantly. In general you may find it like this: if you call upon a man who is busy professionally, and your visit is of no especial interest or object to him, why, frequently you may not be treated very cordially. That was not the case with Dr. Warner. However busy he might be, as far as I know, he was always ready to receive any one and treat him very kindly; and such were all the relations that I ever had with the man. I have seen him here, as the other members have, and there were a good many things about the man, as I look at it, to be admired. If there is anything in a person that I like, it is that openness which Dr. Warner always showed, that willingness to say whatever is thought without any hesitation and without any fear whatever that it will hit in the wrong place, or that offense may be given, or that friends may be lost by the means. Dr. Bowditch has spoken of a certain class of men. He evidently has the same opinion that we all do of a person who is not out-spoken, or who is afraid to speak, or who, just as quick as the back is turned, is going to speak against you. We want to be as free from such a person as possible. It seems to me that it is well for us to consider these different qualities of Dr. Warner's character. And, as far as my own feelings go, I believe we could find no one in the medical profession who would be a better man to follow, as far as life and character are concerned, than the late Dr. Warner.

President W. S. Brown: I am sorry, gentlemen, that so few of the members have come out to-day, but we all know that doctors have not the control of their own time, and I think there can be no doubt that the absent members have been prevented from coming by causes beyond their control.

I was acquainted with Dr. Warner about twenty years. I think it is about twenty years since I first met him; and all my relations with him were of a pleasant and agreeable nature. I can endorse fully the statement of our friend, Dr. Bowditch, that he was not a sneak. He was the very opposite of that. He was an outspoken man. He was not afraid to say what he thought; and, at the same time, he was not afraid to think. He gave his mind full and free liberty. I recollect very well the time when he applied for membership in the Massachusetts Medical Society. Another physician, a much younger man, applied at the same time. The censors had evidently made up their minds to reject them both; and they did manage to confuse the younger man. He stuttered and stammered and finally broke down, and they managed to keep him out. But when Dr. Warner's turn came, undismayed by the failure of the other candidate, he faced the music and passed, as much, I think, by his courage as anything else, because it was evident that he was a man who had studied much earlier than the rejected candidate, and the latter should have been able to answer the questions much better than a man who had studied so much before him. His mere presence seemed to cow the censors. And so he passed the examination. He had presence of mind; in short, he was not put about, and he passed a good examination. The last occasion upon which I had anything to do with Dr. Warner, the last occasion upon which I met him, was a remarkably interesting one; and I do not think I could give the members a better idea of the character of the man, his skill in diagnosis, his courage, his honesty and his generosity than to detail the circumstances of that case. I can do so the more readily because our friend Dr. Marcy was concerned in the same case and can bear out what I have to say. It was the case of a physician's wife here in Boston, who had an abdominal tumor. I had attended her some six or seven years previously for a slight affection; so, when she had been sick a week or ten days, her husband came out to Stoneham and asked me to go in and see her, which I did, that same day. I could not make out what was the matter with her. I went in the next day and made a more thorough examination and failed to make a diagnosis. I then suggested that we call Dr. Warner to see the case, to which the husband was agreeable, and Dr. Warner came. We put the patient under the influence of ether and made a very thorough examination,—a very thorough examination: but we both failed to find out what the nature of the tumor was. The uterus was retroverted, very much so indeed: and the nature of the tumor was obscure. We afterwards, with Dr. Warner's consent, called in Dr. Johnson, of Boston, and again placed her under the influence of ether; but no one of the three could make out what the matter was. Finally, Dr. Marcy, who was away from home at the time, and whom I had sent for previously, arrived, and we made another examination: we then concluded that the only way to arrive at the truth was to make an incision. I had previously sent word to Dr. Marcy that I thought it would be necessary; so he came prepared with his nurse and with all the necessary instruments. He proceeded to make an exploratory incision. I do not intend to go into the history of the case further than to say that the incision enabled us to find out what was really the matter, and that the lady has finally recovered, although I have no doubt in my own mind that if the exploratory incision had not been made she would have died. I simply wish to say that Dr. Warner's conduct in that case was admirable. He said at once, after he had made an examination, "I do not know: I do not know what the matter is."

There are very few doctors who are willing to say that, unless they are pretty skillful. The under class of doctors all pretend to know a great deal more than they do. And it is those who are best informed, generally, who are willing to admit, sometimes, that they do not know what the trouble is. I remember a very good illustration of that in the case of a woman who was tried in Edinburgh for poisoning her lover. My instructor in chemistry was called as a witness, and the counsel who cross-examined him asked him, in view of the fact that she had purchased the arsenic ostensibly for use as a cosmetic, whether it was possible to wash the face with arsenic without inflaming the eyes and spoiling the complexion? "I do not know. I do not know whether it is possible or not," was his prompt answer. That proved the turning point in the case, because the other side had a witness ready to prove that it was possible, who had verified it by experiment. Further than that, when Dr. Warner had made his second visit, the husband of the lady asked him what his charge was, and I shall never forget the way he turned around and said, "What?" He asked again how much he was to pay. Then Dr. Warner said, "Why, we don't do that sort of thing. Dog don't eat dog in our profession." That is about as characteristic of Dr. Warner as anything I could mention.

Dr. H. O. Marcy : Mr. President, there are a great many reminiscences of our friend, Dr. Warner, which, if this were the proper time and place to give them free scope, would be of interest to all of us. I can never forget the many hundreds of miles we have traveled together. Days and days, first and last, we were fellow-travelers in our various journeys to and from the different meetings of the American Medical Association, to which, you know, he was so long and thoroughly devoted, in which association, you know, he had held the second office in its gift, which came to him, it is needless to say, wholly unsolicited. On all these excursions he was the life of the party. Among a dozen or twenty doctors grouped together in the sleeper from morning to night, there was something fresh, original and interesting in Dr. Warner's conversation. Upon whatever topic the conversation turned, he had something to offer that was worth listening to, and that gave profit in the reflection, oftentimes illustrated by the queerest, quaintest, oddest experiences that happen even to doctors. That part of his life, I think, we will all treasure in memory, because that is the easiest to remember.

There is another side of his life which has been referred to by nearly every one who has spoken, and that is the tender solicitude which he had for those in suffering. The best example of it, under my observation, was in the case of our mutual friend, Dr. Didyme, of Syracuse, who, for a number of weeks was ill in my own house this last year. Although there was nothing very especially important in the way of consultation or discussion between Dr. Warner and myself for many days together, yet scarcely twenty-four hours went around that he did not drive out to Cambridge to see him, and if he had half an hour that he could possibly spare, he would sit and cheer up his friend. Dr. Didyme loved him, as did we all. He, like Dr. Wheeler, was an old class-mate of his, in the early days. I suppose, were it possible to have the expression of our profession generally over the country, we should find few men in the United States who were more tenderly loved or remembered more gratefully than Dr. Warner. He came to Boston, as you all know, under peculiarly depressing circumstances, and joined himself to Dr. Storer, at a time when everything seemed propitious, but when, after all, we were just on the verge of a change of public opinion that brought him under the close scrutiny of a critical time. Under all those circumstances, you and I knew him, and he bore himself with remarkable judgment, discrimination and good taste.

I suppose, thus, Mr. President, we could go on and recite the virtues of our friend and brother, were it needful. All of this comes in pleasant remembrance; and it seems hardly possible that he who has been so long with us, who was with us yesterday, is to be with us no more.

The meeting was then adjourned.

Reminiscences.

FROM H. R. STORER, M. D., NEWPORT, R. I.

DR. L. F. WARNER, OF BOSTON.

[For the Journal of the American Medical Association.]

Dr. Levi Farr Warner, for many years an influential member of the American Medical Association, and in 1874 one of its Vice-Presidents, was born October 25, 1822, at Norwich, Chenango County, N. Y. He died upon October 12, 1889, at Boston, two weeks before the completion of his sixty-seventh year. Receiving his early education at the academy at Mexico, N. Y., he studied for his profession during 1842-3 at Geneva Medical College, and subsequently graduated in 1862 at Lind University, Chicago. He commenced practice at Vienna, Oneida County, N. Y., and removed thence to St. Louis, where, during the war, he was Assistant Medical Examiner for the First District of Missouri. He then removed to Boston, and was admitted a Fellow of the Massachusetts Medical Society. He was one of the founders of the Gynæcological

Society of Boston, and soon became recognized as of special skill in the diagnosis and treatment of the diseases of women. He conducted successfully a large practice until his death, which was from cerebral hemorrhagic effusion, the result of an accident.

Though always participating with interest in the discussions at the various scientific societies with which he was connected, he wrote but little, save quite a number of obituaries of deceased members of the American Medical Association. His paper, however, "On the Connection of the Hepatic Functions with Uterine Hyperæmias, Fluxions, Congestions and Inflammations," in the Transactions of the American Medical Association for 1878, vol. xxix, exerted a distinct influence towards obtaining in New England a wider respect by general practitioners for the specialty of gynæcology, then still upon its trial, and at the same time served to curb the somewhat inordinate zeal of a portion of its younger enthusiasts.

The writer of this notice was long associated in practice with Dr. Warner, and the relation was of the most intimate character. From first to last he was always faithful to his duties. Not a shadow of difference ever arose between the two, and there was never an unkind word uttered. Scotch in his parentage, several of the most prominent traits in his character were doubtless inherited. His father a clergyman, he knew the Scriptures absolutely, and they were ever in his mind. He was a Presbyterian from childhood, but toward the end of his life held close relations with the Congregationalists, with whom his lately deceased wife was in communion. He enjoyed, in a pleasant way, religious controversy, but it was rather as a kind teacher than as an antagonist.

He was one of the most genial of men. Full of anecdote to overflowing, cheerful and merry by nature, he carried comfort to the despondent, even when his own disappointments and sorrows, and he had many of them, were weighing most heavily upon him.

He was almost perfection itself in his chosen professional work. Always successful in obtaining the full confidence of a patient, he never proved unworthy. He was untiring, in the most chronic and discouraging cases, to a marked degree. Persistent in following up the instances of this kind that were confided to him, he often produced the most surprising and unexpected cures, restoring women to their full usefulness who had for many years apparently been hopeless invalids. At his funeral there were scores of such, who dated their restoration to domestic happiness and to life itself, a long time back, wholly to him, and who lamented their loss accordingly.

To those who treated him fairly he was devoted in his friendship. He was true as steel and as gentle as a child. "A Scotch saint," he was once playfully called, but the term was no misnomer. Though naturally sensitive and quick tempered, he was always ready to make acknowledgment if it should prove that he had been in error. He disliked to have wealthy patients, declaring that in the middle class one found the most gratitude. To the poor, both in private and hospital practice, he always gave freely of his thought and time, and had he not, beside, contributed much and constantly in other practical charity, he would have amassed a fortune from his profession.

He has left to his friends a better legacy, the loving recollection of a thoroughly upright and honest man, a most delightful companion, an always reliable friend, a really good physician. *May he rest in peace.*

HORATIO R. STORER.

———

From Dr. A. S. Whitmore, Boston, his attending physician: The history of Dr. L. F. Warner's last illness is that of cerebral thrombus. About ten weeks before he gave up he fell from a street car, his foot catching on the rail, which threw him, striking on his knee and shoulder. After this he complained of headache, vertigo, heaviness and drowsiness, frequently falling asleep in his chair with a sentence half completed. A few days before he gave up there was thickness of speech. On the Saturday before he was willing to own he was sick, he assisted at the operation of removing an overian tumor. He said, in one of his lucid intervals: "I wouldn't have undertaken the case for $50,000, but the woman was poor and I wanted to help her (the operation was a success). I was too tired and sick ; it was too much for me ; it was the long road that broke the horse, I guess." On October 1st, 1889, he took to his bed (tending to his patients up to the day before) and I was called to see him. I found him lying upon the right side, face and congunctives red and injected, structerous breathing, pulse sixty, temperature normal. I awakened him quite readily, he recognized me, calling my name, and expressed himself as glad to see me. The usual remedies were ordered, the doctor himself taking an interest and coinciding with the suggestions. After treatment his mind seemed more clear for two days, when he become semi-comatose again. At all times he recognized fellow physicians who came to see him, calling them by name, without their being previously announced, having characteristic remarks for each; he had a good word or joke for all. He continued to be in this state until the evening of October 10th, when symptoms of heart failure developed, finally passing quietly away on the morning of October 12th, this complication being the immediate cause of his death. When rational, he was cheerful and ready with his full fund of wit and quaint sayings, bringing smiles and laughter from those present. I can recall many incidents of this kind. On paper, they would seem tame, but with the personality and short and sharp speech of Dr. Warner. they were always effective in making the sick-room pleasant. He was a man in love with his profession, always seeking for the primary cause of disease, with the persistency and determination characteristic of the man.

A. S. WHITMORE,

No. 1 Union Park.

BALDWINSVILLE, N. Y., Nov. 1, 1889.
MRS. ELLA E. STUART:

Yours of the 25th ult. was duly received. I had heard before of the death of my friend, your respected father, but had very few particulars, and not knowing your address, I had contemplated writing to Dr. Knight, of Boston, for more information. You probably do not recollect me, but I recall you, only as a little girl, at your father's home in Syracuse. But your father I could not forget, for the many thoughtful kindnesses from him received. The friendships of our youthful days by the divergence of our ways and the interests of our business, are generally forgotten before our sun has reached its meridian; but your father is one of the few of my early friends that has never been forgotten, and I am equally satisfied his friendship for me continued during his whole life.

Our acquaintance commenced just fifty years ago last May, when two country youths first met in the halls of Mexico Academy. We were not in the same classes, but our rooms were not far separated; and we soon found ourselves intimate friends. For many years from this, we knew each other's thoughts and plans; and circumstances made by ourselves often brought us together. After completing our scientific course, we commenced the study of medicine in the same office.

In this connection came one of those thoughtful acts of kindness characteristic of him which nothing but the warmest friendship could suggest. For my education I was entirely self dependent. By means

saved by teaching I had got a little more than half
way through my course of medical study when my
means were utterly exhausted. Talking the matter over with him, I was planning to shunt off to
teaching awhile to recuperate my exhausted finances
for I had not a relative to whom I could apply.
He modestly but very pleasantly said, " Kendall,
may be I can help you." In astonishment, I said
(for I had no idea of any but self help), " How can
you help me?" He said that his father (your
grandfather, the Rev. H. Warner), had some money
in the bank which he had refused to lend to several
persons, but, said he, " I guess he'll let you have it."
And so it turned out. In a few days he wrote me
his father would let me have the money; and I
made immediate arrangements for another course of
medical lectures with him. I knew the good Elder
Warner was very friendly, but I know but for your
father's solicitation I never should have had that
money, which would have put me back in my studies at least one year.

Passing over many little acts, scattered through
our lives, I will refer to only one more, so characteristic of his warm heart that I cannot fail to
mention it. A little more than two years ago, I
was lying in bed for many weeks with nervous pros-
tration, caused by many years of professional over-

work. My now departed brother, Rev. Jno. F. Kendall, and wife, came from Indiana to visit me; and it was determined that I should be taken to the seashore, in Maine, for the benefit of the sea air. This took us through Boston; and by my desire my brother wrote to your father that we would get to Boston on a certain train, asking, as we were strangers that he would be at the depot, and give us information about a good hotel near by, where we could stop for a day or two, as I would be too weak to proceed farther. When we arrived there, we found him at the depot not only with needed information, but with nice rooms engaged at the best hotel, an ambulance for me and a hack for the well ones of the party; and while there giving me the benefit of the valuable professional services of himself and of his friend Dr. Knight.

Of such have been the manifestations of kindness of your father since our first acquaintance, a half century ago. Could I do otherwise than respect and love him? I doubt not many others are able to make similar report of the same character. I heard of his sickness a day or two before his death; but when I saw him last he was the picture of health, and I hoped he might recover. But the sad news of his death soon came, and filled my heart with sadness, because I had lost a dear life long friend. You have my warmest sympathy, in this, your irreparable loss. But sympathy can not make up the loss nor fill up the aching void caused by the departure of our dear friends.

Many years of usefulness has he been permitted to spend here, and we hopefully trust he has gone to his reward, where

" Sickness and sorrow, pain and death,
Are felt and feared no more."

Our friends, like ourselves, all have their faults and failings:—let us forget them, emulating their virtues and good works; trusting in the merits of Him who died for us, that we may inherit, by and by, a mansion prepared for those who do His will. When time and circumstances permit, I hope you will write me more fully of your father's sickness and death, and other matters that might be of interest to us.

From your almost unknown, and your father's well known friend,

JAS. V. KENDALL.

FROM PROF. W. H. BYFORD.

CHICAGO, Oct. 28th, 1889.

MRS. STUART:

Dear Madam—Your letter of the 25th inst., bore me the sad news of the death of your estimable father, Dr. L. F. Warner.

My share in the memorial would be to say, "a man of superior professional attainments, an excellent practitioner, a faithful friend, an honored father and husband, a citizen of which his State can be proud, a Christian and an honest man."

Respectfully yours, etc.,

W. H. BYFORD.

DETROIT, Mich., Nov. 15, 1889.

H. R. STORER, M. D.:

My Dear Doctor—I read to-day with deep regret the decease of my old and loved friend Dr. Levi F. Warner. For many years we have met annually at the gathering of the A. M. A., and at Newport we had a most delightful visit together. When in Boston, I always wended my way to the Hotel Pelham to have a gossip with him. And it was with pleasure he spoke to me of the kindly relations that existed between yourself and him. Not knowing personally his family may I kindly ask you to express

to them my sincere regrets at his decease. Early
in life he was only one year my senior and he
should have lived longer for his usefulness. Thus
one by one we pass away, the good unfortunately
being taken first. Please to accept my kindest regards and believe me,

Yours very truly,

WM. BRODIE, M. D.

FROM U. O. B. WINGATE, M. D., MILWAUKEE, WIS.

When a friend passes through that outer portal
of life, called death, we measure our loss by the
impressions made upon us during our associations
in life, and those impressions form an immortal
part which linger in memory, and influence us after
our friend has long passed from mortal view.

The impressions made upon me by the late Dr.
Levi F. Warner are deep and lasting.

As a physician and friend I had known him for
about ten years only, but that was long enough to
feel in a lasting manner the value of his counsel,
influence and friendship. To me he was a father
in medicine, and to me his skill as a physician in
that department in which he was most interested,
while I knew him, was only second to his high sense
of professional integrity and manly honor, a sense

that was indeed refreshing and invigorating to one open to such a noble quality.

In the sick chamber where disease had fastened itself in a serious manner upon the fairest and most sacred of the household and home, and in the council room as a consulting physician, where doubts and fears were wrangling to have full sway, his presence was like an oasis in a desert: fertile, full of hope and cheer, always beaming with new suggestions and possibilities; his presence was life itself both to patient and physician in attendance. A few years ago, just before I left the East to take up my abode in the West, somewhat broken down in health and spirits at that time, due to hard work and the trials incident to life, I called on him at his office in Boston. He loaded me with letters of introduction to members of my profession where I would be likely to go, and wherever I presented those letters they served me at once with a ready passport to any and all medical circles. I did not have the pleasure of seeing him again until a few weeks before his decease, when one bright morning as I sat looking out of my window I heard some one stop in front of my house; on looking to see who the person was, I saw him looking at my door plate; in a second he was ascending my steps; before he could reach the bell I opened the door, and he had me by the hand: "Well, young man, how are you any way, how are you prospering?" Such was his greeting. That evening he dined with me at the medical club, and I spent all the time I could with him during his short stay in the city, for to be in his company was to me an inspiration in my social and professional life, and when I parted from him I felt more than ever the value and grandeur of his friendship.

Our loss is indeed great, but what is our loss is his gain. We cannot wish him back, but such a wish could only be prompted by our own selfishness: we can only mourn our great loss and strive harder to emulate his example in life. His years were full of good deeds. He was the good physician, the steadfast friend, and he died a "grand old man."

U. O. B. WINGATE, M. D.,

204 Biddle Street.

L. F. Warner, M. D., Our Doctor.

He was so good; "but not too good for human nature's daily food."

CAMBRIDGE, Nov. 24, 1889.

MY DEAR MRS. STUART:

I will enclose some extracts from my Sunday reading which have strongly suggested our dear, good Doctor, hoping you also will like them as such: the last one is from an article called "Deacon Herbert's Bible Class"; the subject was "What should be the aim of Life?" One member, who was a physician, thought it should be with him, to "do the greatest good to the largest number of persons, without regard to fees." Another member thought it should be in "doing the duty nearest to one—in cultivating one's own self, all one's influence would become good and true." Objections were raised by the other members, to both of these plans; the first would neglect himself, and the other become selfish; finally, a summary which united both ideas, as here given, was accepted by all the class.

"We never can receive into the secret chambers of our veneration and love any other character than that of the benevolent, the upright and the devout man."

"It is the gospel of cheerfulness that this man unconsciously teaches,—and, a brightness of spirits that makes glad all who meet him."

"What sweet forgiveness, what single aims, what earnest devotions, what discontinuances of pride, and harsh judgments of others, what pure readings and conversings, does almost every one recall in connection with the hour that taught him what is called the mystery of suffering."

"We are to advance the kingdom of God by *bearing witness* to its truth in *word, action* and *life.* The end is a generous one: It is to do the highest good to others, and, in doing them the highest good, we must do them all lower good,—as Jesus healed men's bodies that he might heal their souls, too. But, to do this work requires constant self-culture, also: for we are to bear witness to the truth, and therefore must know it; we must bear witness in life, and therefore must make our life noble. This aim avoids narrowness, for Christ's work was to save all mankind, and so we must take an interest in the whole human race." Dr. Warner seemed all this to me. It did me good, whether I saw him or not, to think of him, as he said once, it was most congenial to him to "go about," in the world, "doing good as Jesus Christ did;" when he came to me and applied himself to my need with tact and sympathy, as well as skill, I realized what was meant by "Jesus touched them." He always asked God, every morning, to direct him aright; and gave thanks every evening for any success that he had found. He had a childlike acquiescence in what seemed to be the Divine Will, and would say cheerfully, "It was all right;" and, he had much deference for the laws of nature—"let nature have her own way! Do just as you feel like doing—lie down or sit up." He was guided by intuition, as well as reason, and, "got along best with those patients who also had it."

You, dear, have been far away from the scene of his activities: While solacing the grief I share with *you*—his only, darling daughter—I would gladly supplement your recollections of him by such as I have. But, first let me observe what a wonderful man he was:—many sided, well balanced. How quick witted and humorous. What method and patience and what nicety, frankness and modesty! What absolute self control! What a sweet disposition! And what a physique! One side of his face was merry and glad in expression, and the other tender and sympathetic. How varied his countenance! How serene and benignant, at times.

5

Those shoulders of his were an assurance of his success, in times of difficulty and depression, giving such a sense of strength.

Those who saw him only when he was in a vivacious mood, as when relieved from anxiety, would have but a limited idea of him. What sensibility he had! How hard it was to see him suffer, especially as he did so with such quiet dignity; but, deary, it widened and deepened his capacity for still nobler enjoyment, because he received it in the true Christian spirit, as for his permanent benefit. The hardest thing that he had to bear, he once said, was when he was called too late, and could not do anything to save life. When he first began practice he went with a physician to visit a patient who was in much suffering; after leaving him he kept talking about him, in his distress of mind; his senior said, in reply: "Young man, when you are older you will get used to such experiences and not think of them again after you leave your patient's door." He said he did not see how that could be, then, and he never had since! The more he suffered himself the more he felt for his patients. He once advised me to go to Dr. B., the aurist, "he is so good," he said, "that you can't help loving him! This, of itself, will do you good!" This could well be applied to himself. I once told him, in reply to his query, and in my comfortable feeling of ease with him, that I felt "very weak, and wished I had a great mother to take me up in her lap." To my surprise, he answered gravely: "We all feel so, sometimes."

To relieve suffering as quick as possible, he often went without his dinner, lost much sleep, took long journeys, was in much exposure to great heat, and in blinding snowstorms, went to poor sick girls, and several times suffered from terrible accidents. It was a relief to one, in thinking of his heroic life, to know what satisfaction awaited him in his home-life and in the companionship of his wife. When I asked if his wife was going with him, as delegate to Halifax: "Oh yes, she went everywhere with him! She read a great deal to him. She was very busy, but never neglected her home. She wanted him to come home early, to take her to ride; but not while he could do any one any good. I must run now; the 'frau' is waiting for me!" He always called his wife "frau," the German for wife.

He often had patients to whom he had to give money, instead of taking any. I asked him, during the late financial crisis, if he was "laying up money for his old age?" "No," he said: "It was hard to get enough money to pay his bills; that one man said he could not take even $25.00 out of his business, without injury;" "but," he added cheerfully, that his " father and grandfather had lived to be very old, and had been] able to work until the last, and he hoped that he should."

During the thirteen years that he attended me, as my physician, I had many opportunities for observing his method of doing. In the usual ten minutes of a medical visit, he dispatched his business without the least sign of the hurry, so injurious to a nervous patient. I remarked to him once, from gratitude, that he never was in a hurry, however brief his time, and he said his (Scotch) grandmother had said, when he was a child, "My bairn, never be in a hurry, except in catching a flea !" Wise grandmother, so to couple her admonition that he would never forget it; for he was very quick, naturally, and full of energy. There, at his grandmother and mother's side, he received some of his early lessons in obedience to a " Divine love." What stories he had in store, suited to all occasions, and how enlivening the cheery ones were for dull times, and there were so many about vigorous folks, when one felt very weak. Then he had such a happy way of dispersing one's fears! I was terrified, once, by finding a smooth, hard lump, the size and shape of an egg, which I felt sure must be a cancer; it proved to be a congestion of a gland, and subsided, under treatment, in a fortnight; some time after I was again alarmed at something of a different nature. "It will all wear away," he said, soothingly as a mother would; and then, the next instant, in a brisk way, he enquired how my cancer was!

Once, there was nothing tangible, only a phantom of trouble in my mind. He perceived it, lifted his eye brows in surprise, and looked very droll about his mouth; I laughed, and it was all over, without a word being said. "I must run," he once said, as he was on his way to Chelsea and Somerville, on a short afternoon in winter. "Why?" I replied, in a playful way, "Have you anything to do?" He immediately assumed a drowsy appearance, (for he was a capital mimic) and said: "No, I want to go home and go to bed!" I once said that "I had thought I should never have a certain kind of suffering again, it had been so long since I had had it." He replied, "Let him that thinketh he standeth take heed lest he fall!" He was a very interesting study, (as an artist would say), under any circumstances. He enjoyed a joke, even at his own expense, as when coming out of his house on a winter's morning, he fell upon some

ice and a neighbor called out : "The wicked stand
on slippery places !"

Once he had just returned from a patient who
was in danger of insanity : I said, "You must
be a good doctor for such, for the worse they feel
the less they can tell any one." He said that a
while before then he "had been called to a poor,
sick girl," who was thus inclined : She looked up
into his face, (so full of benevolence) and asked
if he were her friend ? "To be sure I am," he
cheerily answered ; and then she poured out all
her bad feelings ; her family had been unable to
get her to talk with them, and she had wanted to
be alone. His manners and speech were so cordial
and his temper so equable, that one couldn't help
being drawn to him and feeling faith in his ability
to help one.

Thanksgiving Day: He did me much good
and won my lasting gratitude. It was very sweet
to see him when there was found a permanent
improvement ; he would say, in his open-hearted
way, that he was delighted ; then we would have
a little jubilee in our hearts for ourselves and for
each other. There was one thing in his practice
that was evidently very distasteful, and that was
to offer a bill for the service that he had rendered
so heartily ; I had to make it a study how to make

it agreeable to him. I saw him get out of his carriage once, looking unstrung all over; when he came into my room he was as calm and steady as ever. He had brought his first bill, and this accounted for his dejection. His manner of studying symptoms was remarkable; I think physicians, generally, have a far-away look, as if they were off in their studies; but his was like what I have read of Thoreau's way of studying an animal; and I felt that I was in his grasp (comprehensively) and that he would not relax it until he had done all he could for me.

His practical good sense and benevolence were in constant exercise for many others beside his patients: A poor neighbor "had seen better days;" he used to invite her to dine with him, on Sundays, when he was at home, so that she might have one good dinner during the week. A poor German scholar, who had just arrived, came to him for assistance; he "did not think well to give him money —it would hurt his self respect; so, he got him to give lessons," in his native language, to his wife. A very capable colored boy, of large size, and one who was faithful to him, used to drive for him; one day, I observed a new boy, of small size, and I made some remark about it; "yes," he said, he had discharged the other, but, from no fault of his; he wanted to stay with him and his mother wanted to have him, but the Doctor thought he ought to be in better business, and, he had got him a good place. I wondered if there were many persons who would be so unselfish. Again, he has a colored boy who was with him several years—who, one night, after a revival meeting coming out into the cold night air, was taken suddenly with congestion of the lungs and died in fifteen minutes. The Doctor felt as badly as though one of his own family had been taken; he bought his coffin and paid all expenses and "giving faithful William as good a funeral as any body "—how few would do it.

In keeping pace with this exercise, what an expansion of his manhood—so sturdy to our view—he must have felt! There is a lack of response in some natures, and others seem to crystallize, as it were, at some period of their lives, and ever after to be "so set in their ways," apparently from lack of good, healthy exercise of their faculties; but, he was always pliant; and prompt to adapt himself to others, and, to take a part in the affairs of any circle about him, even in games with little children. He exercised a good deal of hospitality; he did not know how it was, he said, but, he liked to have a good many about him. It must have seemed good to him to be interlocked on all sides of his varied as well as social nature!

He had many grievous trials, but I never saw any trace of bitterness, or of vindictiveness, from them; he seemed, instead, to grow more sweet and wholesome; verily, "Everything works together for the good of those who love the Lord!"

His time for reading must have been very limited; but notwithstanding this, he had a great fund of general information, and had always something interesting to add to any subject that came up; this might partly be accounted for by his quick and comprehensive habit of observation. "I see more than I wish I did, sometimes," he said; then, he had a remarkably retentive memory, although he had so many cares.

He used pithy expressions, at times, especially when praising those he liked; of a patient on Marlboro' street he said, she was "pure gold." I was praising a friend, when he quickly said: "E. H.? She is the salt of the earth!"

He showed me a warm hearted letter from a friend, who said his "latch string was always out for him." He had been to St. Louis, where he had been a Surgeon General during the war, and seen some of his old friends, and had had "such a good time!" He often spoke of Dr. Horatio Storer with much fondness; to go with him to a medical meeting gave him very sweet satisfaction; Dr. S's sons were his also. He was very happy when he told me that his own only son had "experienced *religion*."

He was justly indignant with pretence of all kinds, especially that practiced by quack doctors, and with what was derogatory to dignity and human nature. One day a man came to him with a flattering newspaper puff that he had found, and told him that he "could get that copied into his newspaper," and have it "done cheap," if he would like to have him. His reply was to leave his office at once! He was liable to misapprehension on several points, when it was thought, as one said, on observing his cheerful demeanor, that he was "making lots of money," as if that were his main thought; there was a great mistake.

"Among the distinguished physicians present" at certain dinners and meetings of the profession, who encircled Dr. J. Marion Simms, in New York, would at times be mentioned, "Dr. Warner, of Boston." With a shrinking expression, he said he "did not like to see his name in print;" but he was very much pleased when those who knew and loved him elected him to some honorable position and when they commended him for some active part that he had taken. This seemed to me to indicate that he was much like a woman in his affections.

"The blessing of those ready to perish" rest upon his precious memory.

I am moved, as the dear Quakers would say, to add more emphasis to Dr. Warner's medical manner; Dr. Simms' genius seems to have been employed largely in a mechanical way of helping; but Dr. W's was in his fatherly adaptation of himself: I was "a very sick woman" when he first came to me; there was anguish in my nervous system; a jar would make me fully conscious of it— it, then, seemed as if the nerves were on the outside of me, and that I was confined in a fine wire cage. I was in despair, too; and tender from bereavements. His manner was fitted to me and was like a soft, warm, thick, flexible glove. How? By assuming that I was his child, and calling me so; and, gently and steadily lifting me up to the Infinite Fatherhood! The thought that I was not many years younger than he may cause a smile; but this was what I needed, and, oh how it rested me from the cares and responsibilities of womanhood! And, how he went down into the depths with me, as if he shared in my sufferings; I do not like to speak, or even think, of such dull, private matters, but, how otherwise shall I fairly present "our Doctor?" When he sent me word, by the housemaid, after the first visit, that he had come, it was not in the conventional way,

(that would have made me feel apart from him)
that Dr. Warner had come, but, in the cosy one of
that " my Doctor had come to see me." A sweet little
living text had, for nine years been set before me:
" Of such is the kingdom of heaven; " and, having
studied the childlike spirit, I was ready to follow,
without questioning, within his devout leading-
strings. He was so innocent, so childlike in faith
in the Divine Will.

When I was convalescent I became "Madam!"
Then I ventured to play the part of " Grandmother"
to him—to restore my balance! To this he did
not object.

I felt he lacked in self-esteem, and I set myself
to cheer him. I had read of a fireman, at the head
of a ladder, and about to enter a burning building
to save life, while an awe-stricken crowd watched
below. The man hesitated as the fire above raged
in fury. " Cheer him!" shouted a voice, and there
arose a great clapping, and the intrepid man sprang
forward and rescued a woman. Thus, I felt, " our
Doctor" was often placed; one way in which I gently
tried to do it was to strengthen his self-esteem, for
while he was so capacious and so well developed in
general, he was rather lacking in this quality at
the basis of human nature, but so just was he that
I had to be cautious that I did not offer more at a

time than he could understand was his due. "You think too well of me," he once bravely said. "I am not so good as you think!" But he calmed down when I said in reply, that he "seemed very human, (natural) to me, and trying to be divine," and that this was what I liked him for; he was aware, too, that I had too much reverence for human nature in general, and for him in particular, to take any unworthy advantage of him. This incident was so characteristic of him that I thought I must tell you, even though I had to "expose my hand" in the little game. He would sometimes appear to have more self-esteem than he had, if it were necessary for one's confidence in him, and then he would take some friend's opinion, evidently to support his position with. But when there was no such need, he would speak with a winning frankness, of some sense of insufficiency. I shall cherish his memory and noble example. The world seems much less bright without him, and it will not be so hard to leave it. I long to see tributes to him from some one who can do justice to his genius as a physician, to his capacious manhood so well balanced, his sweet disposition and his genial and equable temper. I am very glad that you could be so much of a support to him during his two latest trials, (his loss of his wife and his own sickness.) It will always be a comfort to you to think of it.

"Blessed are the pure in heart, for they shall see God."

ANNA H. McKEAN,
Cambridge, Mass.

A Tribute from Major B. W. Hubbell, of Medford, Wis.

[To E. E. S., for her Father.]

There is no death, beyond the portal
Of earthly lore, is love immortal.
The thralldom here is but the spirit's night.
Whose prison bars shall change to bars of light.

Endless the chain that links our transient hopes
To Hope's infinitude ; far from the scope
Of blind humanity. On Nature's face
What is. or is to be, no pen can trace.

This is the chrysalis; beyond the tomb
The heart's fond ceaseless longing shall find room.
The greatest wonder of that unknown sphere
Will be to learn how little we knew here.

Dr. Warner's Funeral.

IMPRESSIVE CEREMONY IN THE PARK STREET CHURCH THIS FORENOON.

Funeral services over the remains of the late DR. L. F. WARNER were held at the Park Street church this morning at 10 o'clock. A large number of the medical fraternity had assembled in the parlors of the church, and, as the sad cortege entered the church, joined in the procession. Rev. S. B. Fay and Rev. D. W. Kilburn conducted the services, and at the request of the family of the deceased, Mr. Kilburn delivered the eulogy. The body was encased in a massive casket covered with black broadcloth. The Ruggles street quartet rendered the musical selections. Among the floral tributes was a beautiful design, two hearts of red and white carnations with the words "Soon United" in immortelles. The remains were taken to Milford, N. H., where the burial will take place and where deceased's wife is interred.—*Boston Globe, October 15th, 1889.*

[From the Gynaecological Review, Boston.]

WE regret to announce the death of DR. L. F. WARNER, of Boston, which occurred on October 12, at the age of 67, he being the oldest gynäcologist in active practice in Boston. Very many of our readers will remember him as a regular attendant for many years at the meetings of the American Medical Association. He was a man of singular acumen and penetration and good judgment, of the most indefatigable industry, and unwearying kindness and charity to needy patients. He was endeared alike to his patients by his genuine interest in their welfare, and to his associates by his good-fellowship and unending fund of humorous anecdotes. The immediate cause of his death was a violent cerebral congestion, followed by thrombosis, occasioned by his active participation, as consultant, in a severe case of ovariotomy. He died as he had lived, in the active fulfilment of his professional duties.

I believe my father realized his days were numbered from the date of his fall, and after his knee was healed sufficiently to travel he came to Milwaukee to visit our family, arriving on the 9th of Sept., 1889. Father never looked so well, or was so bright. I had a dream just before he came, in which he told me " he would soon be at rest," and I could not help but worry, but when I saw him looking so well, I felt that we would have him with us for years to come and I was very glad; as I recall the visit from much he said, I know he believed that the end was not far off. He said, " I hope when I die I won't be sick long " and told me " in case anything happened, who to trust, who would be my friend, where to find things," and told me much of his business affairs. All my wishes were gratified at this visit. I had praised my father to all my friends, but few had ever seen him as his visits to us before were necessarily short, but at this time we took a carriage, went over the city, and it seemed to me that he was never so witty and brilliant. I remarked when we got home " That he showed off splendidly." He turned to me with such an appreciative smile, saying, " You are proud of your old father, arn't you ?" I assured him " no one had a better right to be proud than I." He praised my two children, appealing to their self esteem and seemed to enjoy being with them. It has always been a regret to me that they saw so little of him.

Dr. U. O. B. Wingate, of this city, an old friend, gave a supper on the 11th of Sept., at the Medical Society Club, in his honor, which pleased him very much. He spoke with much feeling of the way the fraternity met him and spoke of them all being so enthusiastic in their profession.

I went to Chicago with him and thence to visit his only brother then living. It was very enjoyable to hear the *two boys* tell stories of each other. (This brother died of paralysis two days before father, and what was stranger still, my only brother's wife died the day before, making three deaths in three days.) Father seemed to want to crowd all he could of pleasant events in the time he spent with us, and I was very much depressed when I parted from him, and could not keep the tears back though usually I have been the brave one. On his way home, while visiting relatives in Syracuse, N. Y., he complained of a dizziness, and in his first letter to me he said he was so tired, he guessed he was getting too old to take such long journeys. About a week later he was taken very sick at a friend's house and had to be sent home. He wrote me " I have had a close call, but am feeling better, don't worry." Then came his last letter, he was better but very tired, did not seem to get rested, but was going to take rooms at the Vendome " and would be very comfortable. The truth is, the visit was too short, too much put into too short a time, and I don't get rested." Then came a letter from Dr. Enoch Chase (father's physician for years) saying he called my father a very sick man, but that he would not give up. On the 1st of October I received the summons to go to Boston. My heart fills with gratitude that I could go, and was there in time to do all I could for him and get many words of love and appreciation. One night, he said, " Ella, what do the doctors say is the matter with me?" I told him; I asked if there was anything else that could be done for him? "No, I guess not, I don't know as I can pull through, I would like to live,—I would like to live for my only pet daughter's sake." The night before he died I went into the room bending very near him, when he put his hands on my shoulders, put up his lips for a kiss and said with his own sweet smile, " Bless your heart." Oh blessed words, what a comfort they will always be to me, and what a comfort that I was there and *know* that all that love, attention, skill and money could do was done, and that everything after the decease, was done as he would wish it.

I would like to write *all* the kind and loving things that were said, of the gratitude of his patients as so many said, "we have not only lost our physician but our father, our friend and adviser." All his patients were his children, he had a father's interest in all their welfare aside from their health. I received one letter from which I shall take a few lines and I hope others will not think I am partial. "There are many who owe their lives to him as we most surely do, who must feel that they have lost one of their very best friends. There is not a day passes that we do not recall some kind word or act of your dear father, and it seems harder and harder for us to realize that he is gone from us; I can see him as he sat at his desk so many times when we went in turn to us with his bright happy smile and extending a hand to each of us say, 'Well and how are my two girls this morning?'" They were all his girls.

I am so glad Mrs. McKean speaks of his love and adaptation to children; that was where my father was the most lovely. I don't think any one ever could entertain children as he did. He had a never-ending fund of stories, (fairy stories mostly), and his patience was untiring in repeating them. I think my father was never so happy as when he had dear children clinging all about him, spellbound by

his wonderful fancies. It was a treat that many
older ones enjoyed as well. He was the most lovely, loveable, loving father a child ever had, and my
childhood was delightful. A look, or "Why,
Jimmy!" (he called me by that name when I was
a child,) would check any disposition to do contrary
to his wishes.

Then, I am so glad some have spoken of his
honesty, for he was the very "soul of honor." Not
many know that when I was about twelve years old
I was the innocent cause of his losing the sight of
one eye. Oh! his gentle consideration for my
feelings, scarcely ever speaking of it, or if he did,
would laughingly say "that the doctors said he
could see more with one eye than they could with
two," thus never letting me see he felt his *great loss*.
About that time he signed notes with a friend, and
then came a "financial crisis;" he lost *all* he possessed. Few men would have had the courage to
try and climb the ladder again, crippled as he was,
physically and financially, but he did. He paid
every cent he owed, and every cent the man owed
with whom he signed the notes. When he was
remonstrated with that he did not have to do
it, he said: "I want to stand honorable with all
the world and with my own conscience."

No one knows all the bitter trials he passed

through, always cheerful and without any hard feelings toward those who wronged him, but only kindness and a grieved feeling that they *could* wrong him.

It is a wonder to me he ever accumulated any property, as his heart was so tender toward suffering humanity, and I knew he was always giving. I said to him, "I should think you would give yourself poor." "No, child; as fast as I give out with one hand Providence fills the other; I guess that's the way when a person wants to do right." I must speak of his kindness to inferiors. He always had a pleasant word for every one, all in such a quiet dignity. He used to say, "kind words, such as 'If you please' and 'Thank you' don't cost anything, but cheer people on their hard roads." He always had pleasant words and jokes for those who served him, "because it changes the bent of their thoughts, which was good for them." so he "went about ministering to all" for their good.

I feel so grateful to all who were so kind to me during my stay in Boston, to all the physicians whose busy lives give them little opportunity to think of any outside of their work, but who were never too busy to do all that I wished.

I heard something to-day which pleased me very much; that a Mr. Coburn had donated $5,000 for a bed in the Free Hospital for Women, in Boston, which is to be called "The Dr. Warner Bed." I know how that would please father.

In planning father's head-stone, I felt I would like to show all his friends I appreciate the love they had for him, so I put on the words: " *Our Doctor Sleeps,*" so each friend could feel that *their* love had helped erect a monument to mark his last resting place. I put " Father" on the top, and white pinks, his favorite flower, on the cross. May his body " sleep," but his spirit meet us *all* when " we wake " in that Better Land where part-ings are no more.

ELLA E. STUART.

In the Shadow.

(For the Transcript.)

"All is still—nor cold lips part,
In the room no more is heard
Labored breathing of a heart ;
   Not a pulse is stirred ;
Death has given the noble face
Dignity of loftier grace ;
There he lies—nor watching, weep ;
   Let him sleep.

Wherefore shut the sunshine out ?
All is well. He makes no sign :
He is compassed all about
   With the sun divine.
Yearning skies may o'er him lean.
He is 'rapt with the unseen.
All is well—nor watching. weep ;
   Let him sleep.

No more conflict. no more sighs '
Like a soldier taking rest.
God's beloved, there he lies
On the Eternal Breast.
See the archangel calm and fair '
Would you have him otherwhere?
There he lies—nor watching, weep ;
   Let him sleep."

                         C. E. W. S.